PETER RABBIT'S

Little Guide to Life

10-01
gift

FREDERICK WARNE
Published by the Penguin Group
Penguin Books Ltd, 27 Wrights Lane, London W8 5TZ, England
Penguin Putnam Inc., 375 Hudson Street, New York, NY 10014, USA
Penguin Books Australia Ltd, Ringwood, Victoria, Australia
Penguin Books Canada Ltd, 10 Alcorn Avenue, Toronto, Ontario, Canada M4V 3B2
Penguin Books (N.Z.) Ltd, 182-190 Wairau Road, Auckland 10, New Zealand

Penguin Books Ltd, Registered Offices: Harmondsworth, Middlesex, England

First published 1998

1 3 5 7 9 10 8 6 4 2

ISBN 0 7232 4444 8

Colour reproduction by Saxon Photolitho Ltd., Norwich
Printed and bound in Singapore by Tien Wah Press (Pte) Ltd

PETER RABBIT'S

Little Guide to Life

FREDERICK WARNE

Little Benjamin said, "It spoils people's clothes to squeeze under a gate; the proper way to get in, is to climb down a pear tree."

THE TALE OF BENJAMIN BUNNY

Though Benjamin is correct to preserve his clean clothes, his method for gaining access to Mr. McGregor's garden is rather misguided. The proper etiquette for entering someone's home is to knock on the door or ring the bell and wait to be asked inside. Of course, hungry bunnies will never be welcome guests in a vegetable garden.

Appley Dapply, a little brown mouse,
Goes to the cupboard in somebody's house.

APPLEY DAPPLY'S NURSERY RHYMES

It is terribly offensive to snoop through other people's cupboards.
Rummaging through larders, wardrobes and drawers that do not
belong to you constitutes a gross invasion of privacy. When staying as a guest,
do not help yourself to food from the kitchen. Instead, wait
until you are offered refreshment.

"Mind your Sunday clothes, and remember
to blow your nose . . . Beware of traps, hen roosts, bacon and
eggs; always walk upon your hind legs . . . Observe
sign-posts and mile-stones; do not gobble herring bones . . ."

THE TALE OF PIGLING BLAND

Pigling Bland's mother wants her son to conduct himself with decorum
and reflect his good breeding whilst on his journey. Anyone who
has suffered an uncouth travelling companion will appreciate her
wise list of instructions, though bacon and eggs cause less
worry for humans than for plump little piglets.

The bad Rabbit would like some carrot.
He doesn't say "Please." He takes it!

THE STORY OF A FIERCE BAD RABBIT

The importance of saying "please" before you take something
cannot be stressed enough. Pushing and grabbing is impertinent behaviour,
inexcusable even in a rabbit. Similarly, when someone gives you a
present or performs a favour, always remember to say "thank you."
These short little words speak volumes.

"I will come very punctually, my dear Ribby," wrote Duchess; and then at the end she added—"I hope it isn't mouse?" And then she thought that did not look quite polite; so she scratched out "isn't mouse" and changed it to "I hope it will be fine," and she gave her letter to the postman.

THE TALE OF THE PIE AND THE PATTY-PAN

Invitations often include the initials R.S.V.P., which stand for "répondez s'il vous plaît." This means "please respond" in French. Duchess exhibits proper etiquette by promptly replying to her friend the pussy-cat's invitation to tea. Remember, it is rude to speculate about the menu, even if you suspect that mouse pie will be served.

Sir Isaac Newton wore his black and gold waistcoat. And Mr. Alderman Ptolemy Tortoise brought a salad with him in a string bag.

THE TALE OF MR. JEREMY FISHER

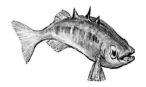

When you are invited to a dinner party, it is polite to arrive on time and wear your best clothes, like Mr. Jeremy Fisher's guests. Always bring a thoughtful present for your host, though flowers or chocolates may be more appreciated than a bag full of lettuce.

"Tiddly, widdly, widdly, Mrs. Tittlemouse; you seem to have plenty of visitors!"

"And without any invitation!" said Mrs. Thomasina Tittlemouse.

THE TALE OF MRS. TITTLEMOUSE

Refrain from making awkward demands on your hostess, such as requesting honey when cherry stones are served. Do not make a mess by tracking wet, muddy footprints into a tidy home. Above all, never be an uninvited guest like Mr. Jackson the toad. Even the most gracious party-givers resent the presence of a gatecrasher.

With the utmost politeness he introduced Timmy Willie to nine other mice, all with long tails and white neck-ties. Timmy Willie's own tail was insignificant. Johnny Town-mouse and his friends noticed it; but they were too well bred to make personal remarks; only one of them asked Timmy Willie if he had ever been in a trap?

THE TALE OF JOHNNY TOWN-MOUSE

A well-mannered host puts his dinner guests at ease, acquaints newcomers with the rest of the company and encourages civil conversation. Courteous guests should eschew making controversial statements and asking inappropriate questions. Do not, for example, suggest that field mice are superior to urban rodents.

The little person made a bob-curtsey—"Oh, yes,
if you please'm; my name is Mrs. Tiggy-winkle;
oh, yes if you please'm, I'm an excellent clear-starcher!"
And she took something out of a clothes-basket,
and spread it on the ironing-blanket.

THE TALE OF MRS. TIGGY-WINKLE

Clean clothes are an essential of good grooming. Nothing is more
off-putting than a handkerchief reeking of onion, muddy stockings or a
jacket stained with blackberry juice. If you do not wish to launder
your clothes yourself, regularly bring them to a reliable
washerwoman such as Mrs. Tiggy-winkle.

Next morning she got up very early and began a spring cleaning which lasted a fortnight. She swept, and scrubbed, and dusted; and she rubbed up the furniture with beeswax, and polished her little tin spoons.

THE TALE OF MRS. TITTLEMOUSE

Always maintain a neat and clean home. A model of good housekeeping, Mrs. Tittlemouse keeps the sandy floors of her home fastidiously tidy and free of cobwebs. A thorough spring cleaning provides an excellent opportunity to scour nooks and crannies and clear out your cupboards, though it need not last two weeks.

And as their eyes became accustomed to the darkness,
they perceived that somebody was asleep on
Mr. Tod's bed, curled up under the blanket.—"He
has gone to bed in his boots," whispered Peter.

THE TALE OF MR. TOD

Going to bed in one's shoes and dirty clothes is a slovenly habit.
If you insist on wearing boots in bed, at least be sure to sleep
between your own sheets. No doubt the smelly, snoring Tommy Brock
will compound the insult by neglecting to wash Mr. Tod's blanket
and make the bed when he awakes.

The customers came in crowds every day and
bought quantities, especially the toffee customers.
But there was always no money; they never paid for
as much as a pennyworth of peppermints.

THE TALE OF GINGER AND PICKLES

Giving unlimited credit is not a sound way to run a business.
The shopkeepers Ginger and Pickles closed their shop because
the customers did not pay. Enormous sales do not signify unless money
fills the till. A sensible businessperson always insists on receiving
payment up front for any goods sold or services rendered.

But Nutkin, who had no respect, began
to dance up and down, tickling old Mr. Brown
with a *nettle* and singing—"Old Mr. B! Riddle-me-ree!. . ."

THE TALE OF SQUIRREL NUTKIN

Squirrel Nutkin, who did not ask Mr. Brown's permission to gather nuts,
shows no deference. People in positions of authority should not be
pestered with insouciant rhymes and teased with impudent antics.
Do not provoke your elders and betters, or you may come to the
same end as Squirrel Nutkin and lose your tail!

Jemima thought him mighty civil and handsome. She explained that she had not lost her way, but that she was trying to find a convenient dry nesting-place.

THE TALE OF JEMIMA PUDDLE-DUCK

Avoid making Jemima Puddle-duck's mistake of trusting strangers,
no matter how elegantly dressed and refined they might appear.
Gullible creatures willing to put faith in strangers usually come to harm.
The gentleman's sandy whiskers and bushy tail should have
instantly alarmed the naïve Jemima.

Timmy Tiptoes sat out, enjoying the breeze;
he whisked his tail and chuckled—"Little wife Goody,
the nuts are ripe; we must lay up a store for
winter and spring."

THE TALE OF TIMMY TIPTOES

Prudent people plan for the future, like Timmy Tiptoes and his wife.
Though you may not need a hoard of acorns, it is highly
sensible to place your money in a bank. A savings account will
allow you to cope with sudden expenses and to
treat yourself on a rainy day.

And because the Mouse has teased
Miss Moppet—Miss Moppet thinks she will tease
the Mouse; which is not at all nice of Miss Moppet.

THE STORY OF MISS MOPPET

Never hurt or torment those less powerful than yourself. Miss Moppet should
have forgiven the disrespectful, but defenceless, Mouse. It is better to exercise
restraint than to exact revenge. Remember, there will always be
someone mightier than you. How would you like to be tied up in a
duster and tossed about like a ball?

Then Tom Thumb lost his temper. He put the
ham in the middle of the floor, and hit it with the tongs and
with the shovel—bang, bang, smash, smash!

THE TALE OF TWO BAD MICE

Violently destroying property that does not belong to you is wrong
and inconsiderate. Stealing, even from dolls, is immoral behaviour.
Tom Thumb and Hunca Munca plunder the doll's house, but later
make amends for the damage and stolen furniture with a
six-pence coin and housekeeping services.

As there was not always quite enough to eat—Benjamin
used to borrow cabbages from Flopsy's brother,
Peter Rabbit, who kept a nursery garden.

THE TALE OF THE FLOPSY BUNNIES

Friends and families should help each other in times of need.
Lend a hand (or a cabbage) to those less fortunate than yourself
whenever possible, especially when resources are scarce. If you treat
needy people with charity and generosity, they will gladly come to
your aid when you experience difficulties.

MORALS

Now run along, and don't get into mischief.
I am going out.

THE TALE OF PETER RABBIT

Children should honour and obey their parents. Old Mrs. Rabbit cautions her offspring
to avoid Mr. McGregor's garden, for she knows that danger lurks amongst the
cabbages and radishes. Naughty Peter recklessly ignores his mother's warning
and nearly suffers the same fate as his unfortunate father. Heed advice given
in your best interest, or you risk ending up in a rabbit pie.